ARMAGEDDON

Novelization by DONA SMITH
STORY BY JONATHAN HENSLEIGH AND ROBERT POOL
SCREENPLAY BY JONATHAN HENSLEIGH
PRODUCED BY JERRY BRUCKHEIMER   GALE ANNE HURD   MICHAEL BAY
DIRECTED BY MICHAEL BAY

Hyperion Paperbacks for Children
New York

Printed in the United States of America

First Edition
3 5 7 9 10 8 6 4 2

The text for this book is set in 14-point Hiroshige.

Library of Congress Catalog Card Number: 97-80398

ISBN: 0-7868-1301-6

CHAPTER ONE

NASA MISSION CONTROL, HOUSTON: 4:47 A.M.
The early morning sky was still dark, but already NASA was buzzing with activity. Flight Director Clark was watching astronaut Pete Shelby on a video monitor. He was talking him through repairs on the space shuttle *Atlantis*.

Dan Truman, the boss, could feel the tension in the air. The repairs were important, and Shelby was having trouble. He was breathing hard.

Truman tapped Clark on the shoulder and motioned for him to move aside. Then he sat down in front of the video screen.

"Pete, this is Truman. Let's try and relax a little, buddy. We've got plenty of time."

"I'm looking good here," Shelby said finally.

Truman didn't have time to breathe a sigh of relief. Suddenly the image on the video monitor spun crazily. The next thing he saw was a picture of the space shuttle being shredded by thousands of tiny speeding pebbles. In seconds it was peeled down to the ribs, as if a flock of angry birds had pecked off its skin.

Truman couldn't believe his eyes. *Whoosh!* A huge fireball roared through the cockpit. *Kablam!* The shuttle exploded.

All the monitors in the room went dead. Everyone stared with shock at the blank screens. Truman's blood turned to ice.

Why? he wondered. What happened? His heart thudded in his chest. He prayed that the shuttle hadn't been attacked.

There was a horrible moment of silence. Then, as if an electric charge had surged through the room, everyone burst into action. Fingers flew over keyboards and voices crackled into telephones.

As soon as the disaster hit, space monitoring equipment all over the world started picking up strange signals.

U.S. SPACE COMMAND: 4:49 A.M.

Operators saw tiny yellow blips appear on the screens in front of them. They didn't know what they were.

"*. . . Sector five-niner is reporting three—now five-eight—I repeat eight unidentified tracks—*"

"*Watchdog, I have four, now nine-make it eleven unknown—I got tracks everywhere—*"

"It could be a surprise missile attack!" yelled the director. "Scramble the Eagles!"

OTIS AIR FORCE BASE, MASSACHUSETTS: 5:03 A.M.

Two dozen pilots and crew raced across the frozen Tarmac to their waiting F-15 Eagles.

They waited for an order to go into battle.

NATIONAL SECURITY COUNCIL SITUATION ROOM, WASHINGTON, D.C.: 5:06 A.M.

Mega-high tech equipment was coming alive. A young aide spoke into one of the three phones he was holding.

"General Kimsey, I have General Vladic from the Russian Air Defense forces. He wants to know what we're doing."

NASA MISSION CONTROL, HOUSTON: 5:09 A.M.

The room was packed. Everyone looked worried. Dan Truman rushed back and forth, barking out orders.

"Hit the log tapes. Maybe it's a glitch. I want NORAD, Space Command, and the 50th Tactical comparing all space junk they track, in every orbit. Check anything and everything! Let's move it!"

Eighty-year-old Dottie stormed outside in her housecoat and slippers. She gripped the flashlight tightly as she marched toward the huge 1920s observatory.

That silly husband of mine is playing astronomer again, she thought angrily. She had had enough of his foolishness.

"Karl!" she screeched as she chugged across the yard. She threw open the door and found the scrawny old fellow peering into a huge telescope.

"It's five-thirty in the morning, Karl! Your chicken pot pie's been on the table for almost ten hours."

Karl kept his eyes glued to the telescope. "This is something new, Dottie," he said. "Go get my phone book."

"*Excuse me,*" Dottie said angrily. "Am I wearing a sign that says 'Karl's Slave'?"

Karl whirled around and shouted, "Go get my phone book!"

A military motorcade raced toward the White House. USAF Lt. General Kimsey, chairman of the joint chiefs of staff, sat inside the limousine. His deputy was beside him.

"Space Command is reporting negative, that is zero global launches," said the deputy. "It might be pieces of the shuttle reentering the atmosphere causing false readings."

"Yeah, and it might be Santa Claus," General Kimsey replied grimly. "We've got to know for certain that it's not an attack. Driver, let's speed it up!"

NEW YORK CITY: EARLY MORNING

The heart of the city was beginning to pump. A bulldog and his owner walked along a busy street, past people reading newspapers. The headlines blared, SHUTTLE MISSING! DISASTER IN ORBIT!

8

They stopped in front of an electronics store, where a crowd had gathered. Inside the window, televisions were broadcasting news reports about the shuttle.

The bulldog strained at his leash. *What's going on?* he wondered. *Something's up. I can feel it. Uh-oh. I hear the call of nature.*

The dog lifted his leg and a huge sonic boom roared overhead.

Screams filled the air as the crowd scattered. The rock slammed into the pavement where the big guy had been standing.

Yikes, the sky is falling, the sky is falling, the bulldog thought.

The televisions were blown sky-high in an explosion of metal and glass. The store window shattered. Drivers jammed on brakes and leaned on horns as people raced into the streets.

A rock the size of a dump truck streaked through the sky and blasted through three huge buildings. More rocks zoomed down.

Bricks and mortar crumbled as the top five floors of a building toppled to the ground.

Boulders exploded down on an intersection. Cars were flew through the air, inches over people's heads.

Then suddenly it was over. A heavy silence hung in the air, broken only by the hissing of steam.

A crater ten feet wide and forty feet deep had been gouged in the electronics store. A still-smoking, red-hot meteorite lay at the bottom of the hole.

Ruff! Ruff! Hey, somebody help! I'm down here!

The dog's owner peered over the edge of the crater. Far down he could see his bulldog. His leash had caught on something.

"Hang on, Little Richard!" he yelled. "I'm calling nine-one-one!"

CHAPTER TWO

A technician hurried over to Dan Truman. "Sir, it was a meteor shower in the northern hemisphere!"

"Stay focused," Truman said. "We need to know where the thing is headed."

"That could take a week to—"

"Just do it," Truman said quickly. I need to know if the worst is over, or on its way."

Another tech handed him a phone. "General Kimsey is calling from the National Security Council in Washington."

Dan Truman took the phone. "Truman here."

"We got hits from Finland to South Carolina. We know they aren't missiles. So what are they?" the general demanded.

"Meteor shower," Truman explained. "That's what took out the shuttle.

"Is it over?" barked the general.

Dan Truman felt a prickle of annoyance. "The sooner I get off the phone the sooner I'll know. I'll call you back." He hung up the phone before the general could say anything else. He wanted to get back to work.

But he didn't have a chance. He had to take another phone call. This time it was from someone named Karl. He was calling from his trailer in Arizona.

Dan Truman listened as Karl babbled on about seeing an explosion in space. This guy sounds like a nut, he thought at first. The more he listened, though, the more he realized that Karl had seen the meteor shower and maybe something bigger.

"Karl, I'm counting on you to keep this to yourself," Truman told him. "Top secret, understand?" The last thing he wanted was for Karl to start blabbing to the newspapers. There would be panic in the streets.

Karl felt very important. He sat up straighter.

"Yes, sir," he said. "I'm retired navy. I know what 'classified' means—but one more thing: the person who finds her gets to name her, right?"

"Right," Truman agreed quickly. He was too busy to talk to Karl anymore.

"I wanna name her 'Dottie' after my wife," Karl said.

Dottie, who was listening, smiled. But the smile vanished from her face a moment later, as Karl continued.

". . . She's a vicious, life-sucking witch, and there's no escaping her."

Dan Truman was glad to get rid of Karl. Ten minutes later he was standing in the conference room filled with scientific experts.

He was talking to the president, who was calling from Air Force One.

The president wanted answers right now. "Enough with the scientific gobbledygook, Dan. Tell me exactly what's causing all the trouble." His voice came through the speakerphone.

Nobody in the room moved a muscle. They were barely breathing.

"It's an asteroid, sir," Truman said. He looked down at the pictures of the gigantic ball of dirt and ice.

"How big are we talking?" the president asked.

One of the experts spoke up. "Our best guess is ninety-six point five billion cubic kill—"

Truman waved his hands in the air. Might as well keep it simple, he thought. "It's the size of Texas, Mr. President."

General Kimsey got on the line. "What about this morning? How big were those?"

"Nothing—pebbles—the size of basket-balls and small cars," Truman replied.

"Is this thing gonna hit us?" the president asked. "What kind of damage would it do?"

Truman took a deep breath. There was no way to make the answer sound good, so he decided to give it to him straight. "Total damage, sir. This is what we call a global killer. The end of mankind. Doesn't matter where it hits, nothing would survive. Not even bacteria."

Suddenly, the door across the room opened. A guy holding a printout stood there. He was a math whiz, and he had been figuring out how much time was left before the asteroid hit the earth. One look at his face and Truman knew he had bad news.

"How much time?" Truman asked.

"We have eighteen days."

CHAPTER THREE

Dan Truman looked across the conference room table at General Kimsey. I hope we can get him to go along with our plan, he thought. It's our only chance.

Truman and his crew were exhausted. They had studied drawings, books, and reports, made sketches and scale models. General Kimsey had flown in to hear how they were going to stop the earth from being wiped out. He had some ideas of his own.

"Why don't we just send up a hundred and fifty nuclear warheads and blow that rock apart?" Kimsey asked.

"Good question. Bad idea," someone said.

Kimsey gave the guy a withering look. "Was I talking to you?"

Uh-oh, thought Truman. The general just insulted a genius. He hurried to smooth things over.

"General Kimsey, this is Dr. Ronald Quincy from Research." He introduced the two men. "Dr. Quincy is pretty much the smartest man on the planet. You might want to listen to him."

"You could hit this target with all the nukes you want and she'd just smile at you," Dr. Quincy told the general.

Kimsey drew himself up. "You should know the president's science advisers suggest a nuclear blast could change the asteroid's direction."

Quincy pushed his objection aside. "I know those advisors. We all went to MIT and I can tell you, in a situation like this you do not want to listen to a man who got a C-minus in astrophysics. His advisers are wrong."

General Kimsey looked shocked. He wasn't used to having people disagree with him.

"Hitting the rock from outside won't do the job," Dan Truman explained. "If you set a firecracker off in your open palm you get a burn. But close your fist and light that fuse . . . and your wife's gonna be opening the ketchup bottle for you the rest of your life."

"You're suggesting we nuke the thing from *inside*?" the general asked with amazement. "How?"

Here we go, thought Truman. He laid out the plan. "We drill a hole in it. We bring in the world's best deep core driller . . ."

Harry Stamper, the world's best deep core driller, was covered in greasy black oil. A gusher had just drenched him and his whole crew. They were all standing on the deck of the offshore oil rig feeling grimy and tired.

Harry heard the *whok whok whok* of a helicopter propeller and looked up in the sky. A Seahawk was flying toward the rig.

Moments later the helicopter landed. The doors flew open and six armed marines got out, followed by a man wearing plenty of brass.

"Who's Harry Stamper?" the man asked.

Harry stared in disbelief. "Over here!" he called. He wondered what in the world was going on.

The man walked over to Harry. "I'm Admiral Kelso, commander of the Pacific fleet" he said. "We need to talk privately."

Harry followed Admiral Kelso into the roar of the helicopter's rotor wash. The rest of the crew couldn't hear them over the noise.

"I've been sent here by the secretary of defense on direct orders from the president of the United States. This is a matter of urgent national security. I need you to get on this chopper right now, no questions asked."

Harry couldn't believe his ears. Someone must be playing a practical joke on me, he thought. "Did Crazy Willy put you up to this?" he asked.

Admiral Kelso didn't crack a smile. "I'm afraid I don't know Crazy Willy. I'm dead serious about this."

Everyone was staring at Harry and the admiral. It was beginning to dawn on Harry that this was real.

He looked at his daughter, Grace. She was a pretty young woman in her early twenties and she meant the world to Harry. Grace had just told her father that she was in love with a crew member named A. J.

The news had made Harry fighting mad. He was sure that A. J. was all wrong for Grace. He was too wild—too much like Harry had been when he was young. He was sure Grace would be better off without him. Harry glanced at A. J. and suddenly he got an idea. He turned back to the general and said, "I'll go with you on one condition."

A moment later four marines walked

over to where A. J. and Grace were talking. "Miss, you're requested on board. It's a matter of national security."

"National security and you want me?" Grace asked, surprised. She and A. J. exchanged confused looks.

Suddenly two marines grabbed A. J. Then two others grabbed Grace and began pulling her toward the chopper.

Harry smiled as Grace was "escorted" into the helicopter. He'd gotten his daughter away from A. J., at least for now. He looked down at Chick, his right-hand man.

"Chick, you're in charge!" he yelled. "Send the guys home!"

He waved good-bye as the chopper took off.

CHAPTER FOUR

TIME TO GLOBAL IMPACT: SEVENTEEN DAYS
"This is unreal," Harry said. He and Grace were sitting at the table in the conference room at Mission Control. Dan Truman and Dr. Quincy had just told Harry that he was part of a plan to save the earth from being demolished.

"Mr. Stamper, this is as real as it gets," Dan Truman said. He explained what had caused the meteor shower. "A rogue comet hit an asteroid belt. The asteroid is coming at us. Right now. At 22,000 miles an hour. And none of us . . . anyone, anywhere . . . can hide from it."

Truman swallowed. He didn't even like to talk about what would happen if the asteroid landed on earth. "Even if this asteroid hits water, it's still hitting land. It'll flash-boil millions of gallons of seawater and slam into ocean bedrock. A Pacific impact and a tidal wave three miles high travels a thousand miles an hour, covering California, washing up in Denver. Japan. Gone. Australia. Gone. Half the world's population gets burned by the heat blasts. The rest freeze to death from nuclear winter."

Harry's mind was reeling. "I take it . . . you're not alerting everyone about this."

Truman nodded. "No one knows. And that's how it stays. If news like this broke there would be worldwide panic."

Harry looked at him thoughtfully. "So there are six billion people on the planet and you call me. Why?"

Truman and Dr. Quincy exchanged glances. "Follow me," Truman said after a moment. "I have something to show you."

Harry and Grace headed downstairs

along with Truman and Quincy and a military escort. Truman continued to explain as they walked.

"We want to land on the asteroid, drill a hole, drop in some nukes, take off, and detonate. Except we have an equipment problem."

That's not the only problem you've got, Harry thought. They reached the NASA research and development hangar. Two armed guards opened the doors and let them pass.

Harry's jaw dropped when he saw what was inside the hangar. It was an oil rig with a huge robotic drilling arm and a mass of complex machinery, gears, and Teflon cables. He had designed it himself.

Harry circled the thing in amazement. How did they get hold of this? he wondered. Then he realized that they must have taken the blueprints from the patent office. No one had even told him.

"You may recognize the rig," Quincy said nervously. He said something about building it to drill for water on the moon. Harry barely heard him.

He stared at Truman and Quincy. "I got dragged into this because you stole from me?" Harry shook his head. "You did a lousy job of putting it together. And by the way, who's been operating this thing?"

Truman called across the room and eight NASA mission specialists began walking toward them. They look like the geek patrol on parade, Harry thought. Nerdnauts. "What's this?" he asked.

"We've had them training for eight months," said Quincy. "Now we need you to fine-tune the equipment and finish training this team."

Harry could barely keep from laughing. "Eight whole months. Gosh. I've been drilling since I was twelve years old. It took me thirty-two years, every day, every minute, to learn what I know. I'm the best and I work with the best. In seventeen days

I couldn't teach these Trekkies any more about drilling than you could teach me to fly a spaceship."

"You got any other ideas?" Truman asked.

Harry thought for a moment. He figured the only way he could pull this off was with his own bunch of guys. They knew more about drilling than the NASA geeks—but they weren't astronauts.

"All they have to do is drill, right?" he asked Truman. "No spacewalking, no crazy astronaut stuff?"

"Uh, yeah, *just drill*. On an asteroid flying twenty-two thousand miles an hour!" Grace added.

"Then we drop the bomb, take off, and detonate," Harry continued.

"That's the plan," Truman agreed.

"And if it doesn't work, we all die anyway," Harry said.

Truman looked him right in the eye. "All of us. Everywhere," he said.

CHAPTER FIVE

Harry's crew walked into Mission Control laughing and joking. What a weird-looking bunch, Dan Truman thought. The seven guys were full of tattoos and bad attitudes.

"You'd better tell me what's goin' on," said Harry's old pal Chick.

"What's up, Harry? NASA found oil in space?" asked the one called Bear, who looked like his name.

The rest of the guys waited to find out why they'd been dragged to the space center. A. J. was there too. Harry had asked him to come himself. It was the last thing he wanted to do, but A. J. was one of the best drillers around, and he needed him.

Dan Truman turned off the lights and

began showing pictures of the asteroid. He explained what would happen if it hit the earth. Then he told the guys why they were there.

When the lights went up the guys weren't laughing and joking anymore. They looked stunned.

"Does anyone have any questions?" Truman asked.

"Yeah, you got the right guys?" Max piped up.

"Is this a joke?" asked Noonan, the Australian.

Rockhound, the geologist, just sat there looking spaced-out.

Harry studied the faces of the guys he knew so well. He turned to Truman. "I need to talk to 'em. Alone."

Truman, Kimsey, and the NASA techs walked out of the room. While they waited in the hall, Truman and Kimsey skimmed through the guys' files.

"The future of the planet depends on a group of misfits I wouldn't even trust with a potato gun," General Kimsey said after a moment.

"Sir, they're the best at what they do," Truman replied.

Suddenly the conference room doors opened. Harry walked out first, with the guys behind him.

"What's the verdict?" Truman asked.

"The guys will do it, but they have a few requests," Harry replied.

"Like what?"

Harry unfolded a list and began to read. "Oscar's got some outstanding parking tickets he wants wiped off his record." Truman took the list from Harry and skimmed it. "I'll agree to these demands," he said quickly.

Rockhound cleared his throat and motioned Harry over. He whispered something in his ear.

"One more thing," Harry said. "They don't want to pay taxes. Ever."

Dan Truman groaned. The guys had him over a barrel. He had to get these guys into space or it wouldn't matter what they wanted.

"Failed, failed, totally failed." Dr. Banks, head of the medical team, pointed to the files that contained the guys' records.

Harry and the other guys had just finished taking their physicals.

Dan Truman gave Dr. Banks a long look. He didn't want anything to hold up this mission. "Can they survive the trip?" he asked. "That's all we need to know."

"I don't even know how they survived the tests," said Dr. Banks. He looked at Dan Truman's face and let out a sigh. He began stamping a big red APPROVED over the black letters that read FAILED.

CHAPTER SIX

"Good morning," Colonel Sharp said to Harry and his crew. "United States astronauts train for years. You have twelve days. Gentlemen, we are up the creek without a paddle, and the creek's full of alligators."

Colonel Sharp marched them all out to the hangar where Dan Truman was waiting with Dr. Quincy and a military staff. When the hangar's giant doors opened, the guys all gasped. It was the first time they had seen the X-71 space shuttle. A truly awesome sight, it was incredibly huge and high-tech.

While the guys gawked at the shuttle, Truman explained the mission.

"You'll be divided into two groups. Air Force Colonel Davis and NASA Pilot

Tucker will command the red team on the shuttle *Independence*. Air Force Colonel Sharp and NASA Pilot Watts will command the blue team on the sister ship, *Freedom*."

At first Harry and the guys were surprised that Watts was a woman. They hadn't figured on a female pilot. But then they thought, why not? Then Truman introduced the bomb specialists, Gruber and Halsey.

"Once you land on the asteroid," Dr. Quincy explained, "you'll be using our very special drill unit. We call it the Monster Armadillo."

Catchy name, thought Harry. But it's not *your* drill, it's *my* drill.

From that moment on, the guys barely had time to breathe. When they weren't getting the drill ready, they were in flight training.

"I will suck your eyes to the back of your heads, flip you, spin you, and splat your bodies till your bones hurt," promised

Look out below! A meteorite slams into the streets of New York City.

Harry, A. J., and the crew, hard at work at the oil field—doing what they know best.

A. J. loves Grace—no matter *what* Harry thinks.

Harry must convince his crew to risk their lives to save the planet.

"There's no room for mistakes," Harry tells his men.

Grace and A. J. say good-bye—maybe forever.

The fate of the planet rests on their shoulders.

Every second counts as the remaining crew tries to get the Armadillo working.

The Armadillo goes to work on the asteroid—without a second to spare.

Grace waits in agony for news about her father and A. J.

Truman and Clark count down the minutes to Zero Barrier.

Harry says good-bye to Grace before disconnecting the video link.

"I win," says Harry as he takes one last look at Earth.

trainer Chuck Jr. He wasn't kidding.

The guys were crammed into T-38s and flown on roller coaster rides that turned their insides to jelly. They were plunged into underwater tanks until they were soggy.

Then there was the "vomit comet." It earned its nickname from the way it made you feel.

Through all the training, Harry kept thinking of the mission. It was going to be tough, and they had to succeed.

"What are you thinking, Harry?" Rockhound asked after they had been training for several days. They were in a wind tunnel. It felt kind of like being caught in a tornado.

Harry looked at the whizzing blades of the fan. "I'm thinking that as bad as it gets down here . . . up there they don't have an 'off' switch."

TIME TO GLOBAL IMPACT: SIX DAYS

CHAPTER SEVEN

"Both shuttles take off Tuesday at 8:14 A.M.," Dan Truman told Harry and the rest of the guys. He and the NASA staffers had gathered them together at Mission Control to give them an overview of the flight plan.

"Twenty-seven minutes after takeoff the shuttles will dock with the Russian space station to refuel," he went on. "Then you'll start your sixty-hour trip toward the moon. We've only got one shot at landing on the rock and that's when it passes by the moon. Then you'll use lunar gravity to double your speed. We're gonna slingshot you around the moon."

"I remember this one," said Harry. "The coyote sat in a slingshot with a rocket strapped to his back. It didn't work out too well in the cartoon."

"You'll have a better rocket than the coyote had, Stamper," Truman replied. "You'll be traveling at 22,500 miles an hour. You'll come around behind the asteroid and land right here." He pointed to a spot on the map beside him. "That's it."

Good luck, thought Harry. We're gonna need it.

"Let's say for a second we actually land on the thing. What's it gonna be like?" asked Oscar.

"Two hundred degrees in sunlight, minus two hundred in shade," Truman replied. "Canyons of razor-sharp rock. Unstable ground, unclear gravitational conditions, unpredictable eruptions . . ."

"Thanks," Oscar cut him off. He looked a little green. "All you had to say was 'scariest environment imaginable.'"

Truman moved to a monitor and hit his

remote computer control. An image of the asteroid appeared on the screen.

"You drill, you drop the nuke, you leave. Now here's the key: you'll remote-detonate the bomb before the asteroid passes Zero Barrier. You do that and the remaining pieces of rock will slide right by us."

The display showed two giant asteroid halves just missing the earth.

"If the asteroid passes Zero Barrier and the bomb hasn't exploded, the game's over."

They all watched with dread as the monitor displayed the bomb discharging past Zero Barrier—and both halves of the asteroid hitting the earth.

Truman faced the group. "If you don't make it, you can't quit and go home. Because you won't have one."

CHAPTER EIGHT

"All right, we're going down for a bit change! Bear, clamp it down! Hurry, hurry, hurry!" Harry urged. He stood in the monitoring room, stopwatch in hand as the red team went through a practice run in the water tank. Truman and Sharp looked on as A. J. tried to adjust the mock drill arm.

"You guys gotta do this faster up there!" Harry called out. "Load the pipe, Oscar. A. J., let's up the torque."

Truman was praying the exercise went well. They were up against incredible odds. If the mission succeeded, it would be a minor miracle.

The guys were sweating inside their helmets. They were racing against the clock, drilling and pulling cable and clamping pipe.

"A. J., pull back to eight thousand RPMs," Harry yelled to him.

"We don't have time for eight thousand RPMs" A. J. yelled back.

Harry could feel his blood heating up. "Take her back or you'll snap the pipe or blow the tranny!"

A. J. wouldn't listen. "Come on guys, keep it up!" he urged. "I'm going to eleven thousand RPMs. Bear, give the turbine more O2!"

The drill started to shake. "Harry, are you listening to this?" Bear asked.

"Harry, are you listening to this?" A. J. echoed, mimicking him. "Bear, you listen to *me*."

Harry's eyes shot daggers at A. J. "Back off *now*, A. J.! You're gonna blow the tranny!"

"Keep it going, Bear!" A. J. commanded. You're on *my* team."

Suddenly, needles on meters started jumping. An alarm went off. The tranny blew.

"Get A. J. out of there! Pull him up!" Harry said furiously.

A. J. was hauled from the water. As soon as Harry got his hands on him he slammed him against the wall. *"Your team? Your team* just blew the transmission."

"That NASA wimp computer's *wrong*," A. J. argued. "Your drill can take it."

His words only fueled Harry's anger. "That rock's not the place to find out! There's no room for hot-dogging, showing off, or trying to be a hero. You got that! Tell me you got it! Say the words!" Harry glared at him.

"I got it! I got it!" A. J. gave in.

Harry's eyes bored into A. J. "I want you to go back in there and do it my way, no fight, no ego, no questions asked."

This time the team did things Harry's way. It worked.

CHAPTER NINE

The night before the guys were set to go, Chick went to see his son, Tommy—a boy he hardly knew. Harry went to visit his father.

Hollis Stamper was old but he was still tough. He lay in bed, watched over by full-time nurses.

"They treating you all right, Grap?" Harry used his father's nickname.

The old man looked up at him. "Pills every four hours. Jell-O every five," he grumbled. "You know what Jell-O is? It's pudding for sissies."

"They give it to you because it's good for you," Harry told him.

"I'm ready to work. You got a job comin' up?"

If you only knew, Harry thought. "Yeah, we got one."

The old man's eyes sparkled with excitement. "I got my boots and gloves. I'm all packed and ready for a mud hunt."

Harry felt a tug at his heart. He stood there looking down at his father. "I love you, Grap," he said after a moment.

The words caught the macho old fellow off-guard. For a moment he looked misty-eyed. Then his usual bluster returned. "Prove it, then!" he thundered. "Go get me some *real* pudding!"

When Harry got back to Mission Control he found the place in a mad scramble. The room was alive with activity and phones were ringing off the hook.

"What's going on?" Harry asked a NASA staffer.

"They've spotted more incoming," came the quick reply.

Harry was stunned. Another rock was headed toward them. What kind of damage would this one cause? he wondered.

Dan Truman was at the center of the crisis. "Give me a projected impact!" he barked at a technician.

"East Asia. Eleven minutes."

"We've got to warn them," Flight Director Clark said.

"Warn who?" Truman replied. "The entire South Pacific?" He knew that nothing anyone could do would help. They could only wait.

They didn't have to wait long. Minutes later the asteroid plunged into the ocean. Millions of gallons of sea water were flash-boiled instantly. Boats were ripped apart.

There was dead silence in the room. Everyone was thinking the same thing. If the big one hit the earth the damage would be much worse. It would be total.

Truman walked over to Harry. "Do me a

favor and tell me you've never let anyone down."

"Well . . ." Harry hesitated.

"Just say it, even if you have to lie."

"I've never quit. How's that?" Harry asked.

Truman almost smiled. Then he sighed. "I'd be on that shuttle with you, Harry. If I could."

"You don't want to go up any more than I do," Harry said. "You're afraid, 'cause you don't really know what we're up against."

Truman shook his head. "No. I'm afraid . . . because I think I do."

CHAPTER TEN

This is it, Harry thought, as he and his men began to suit up for the space flight. He was glad that he and Grace had had a heart-to-heart talk earlier. Grace had told him that she and A. J. were engaged.

The news didn't make Harry happy. But he had decided it was no time to argue, so he promised her that he and A. J. would both come home.

It was time to go. Tons of NASA techs were scurrying around. The area was loaded with military security.

Harry watched as Grace and A. J. said their good-byes. A. J. suddenly burst into song. The other guys joined in.

Then security held the news crews back

as the men boarded the vehicles that were going to take them to the shuttles. The convoy was guided down the three-mile road by five police cars. Three NASA Huey helicopters loaded with SWAT teams flew overhead.

The sun was setting. People all over the world were glued to their television sets. While the president talked to the country, pictures of the guys getting into the spacecraft flashed on the screen.

Chick's son, Tommy, was surprised to see his father on TV. Now he and his mom knew what he meant when he had told them they'd be proud of him. The whole world was depending on this bunch of guys.

Moments later, strap-in teams were harnessing Harry, Chick, Max, and Rockhound in the shuttle *Freedom*. Up front, Sharp, Watts, and Gruber were prepping final checks. In the *Independence*, A. J., Noonan,

Bear, and Oscar were also being strapped in.

The countdown began:

Ten . . .

Nine . . .

Eight . . .

In the shuttles the guys were trying to keep calm. Some took deep breaths. Some closed their eyes. Some prayed.

Three, two, one . . . .

"We have main engine start," Sharp relayed the message back to the control room.

Liftoff . . .

There was a roar as the shuttle engines fired. Huge clouds of smoke billowed over the ground as the gigantic rockets cleared the launching pads. *Freedom* and *Independence* screamed away from Earth.

CHAPTER ELEVEN

"Fuel teams prepare to unload," Sharp radioed the crew.

The blue of the earth's atmosphere had faded into the blackness of space hours ago. Now it was time to dock at the Russian space station and refuel.

The two shuttles approached the space station's twin docking ports. As they entered the docking module, Lev, the Russian cosmonaut, popped out of a hatch. He had a wild look in his big dark eyes.

"Welcome," he said in English with a thick Russian accent.

"I'm Colonel Sharp," said the commander of the mission. "We should start fuel transfer immediately."

Lev had something to say first. "Your plan for breaking the asteroid into two pieces is not possible."

Sharp didn't have time to argue. "We have only thirty-five minutes to refuel. Let's hurry."

"I am not a gas station," Lev replied. Then, without warning, his knees buckled and he fell down. The guys stared in surprise.

"Space legs," Lev sputtered in his heavy Russian accent. He scrambled to his feet and wobbled away.

The crew followed Lev into the lower cell pod of the space station. It was cramped and moldy, and cluttered like the glove compartment of an old car. Pipes and tubing snaked everywhere.

"You will be below, observing pressure gauge," Lev told A. J. He helped him put on a heavy suit to protect him from the cold. Then he led him down a twenty-five-foot shaft into a frosty room lined with huge tanks.

Lev moved to the fuel gauge. "See gauge? You watch," he told A. J. "One fifty, good. One sixty, good. Two hundred? Very bad. Disaster for space station." He pointed to an intercom. "You tell Lev before it gets very bad."

He showed A. J. the steel shut-off valve. "If past two hundred, pull this lever." Then he headed back up the ladder.

On the upper deck of the space station the two teams were working furiously to refuel the shuttles. They were pumping negative 400-degree liquid oxygen through hoses.

"How long have you been alone up here?" Rockhound asked Lev.

"Eighteen months," Lev replied. "It was supposed to be for only ninety days. I am lonely a lot."

Down below, A. J. watched the fuel gauge, which was starting to rise. He spoke into the intercom. "Lev? The pressure's climbing."

Up above, only a crackle of static came out of the speaker. The guys who were working and talking didn't even notice. The green lights on the control panel were quickly changing to red.

Down below, A. J. was getting worried. The gauge climbed to195, and then to 200.

A. J. pulled the lever on the shut-off valve. But it broke off in his hand. The liquid oxygen oozed into a circuit board. Sparks showered A. J.

There was a brownout in the entire space station. For a moment everyone was very quiet. Then Lev realized what had happened. A look of horror came over his face.

"Get out! Get out! Get out!" he screamed.

Panic erupted. Sharp snapped out orders. "E-vac! E-vac! Prepare to unhook shuttles! Move!"

The alarm sounded. A warning message

blared over the speakers—in Russian. A. J. hurried up the ladder.

By the time he reached the next level, sparks were popping everywhere. Lev raced toward him.

"What happened?" A. J. screamed. "I called you!"

"Why didn't you use the shut-off valve? Why didn't you pull the lever?" Lev screamed back.

A. J. held out his hand. "Here is the lever," he said, showing Lev the broken piece.

While A. J. and Lev were arguing, the others were on the upper deck, scrambling toward the shuttles. Colonel Sharp watched the flames shooting from the space station and the sparks crackling in the air. They had to get out of there fast. The space station was going to explode.

Sharp closed the hatch behind him and hurried toward the *Freedom*. A. J. and Lev were trapped inside the space station.

CHAPTER TWELVE

"This thing won't budge," A. J. said. He and Lev gave the hatch another push. It didn't open.

Then Lev thought of another way out. They could go through an air shaft. He popped open the door, and freezing cold vapors poured in. The air shaft wasn't heated and the temperature was minus one hundred degrees.

"Hold breath or lungs will freeze. And touch nothing," Lev gasped before climbing in. A. J. took a deep breath and plunged into the shaft behind him.

The space was so tight they had to crawl along on their elbows, and so cold that A. J. thought his bones had turned to ice. His lungs cried out for air.

Breathe and you'll die, he told himself. Somehow he made himself go on.

Meanwhile, the rest of the crew was wondering what had happened to A. J. and Lev. Harry was standing in the docking port outside the *Freedom*, going nuts. Time was running out.

"Let's push off," said Commander Watts.

"We gotta make sure they get back!" Harry yelled.

"There's no time!" said Colonel Sharp. "Get inside before this whole thing explodes!" Sharp ordered.

Gruber, Chick, and Max pulled Harry into the shuttle.

"Fire her up!" Sharp ordered Tucker. He pushed a button on the console and the doors slid shut. "Full thrusters!"

Boom! Boom! Boom! A noise like hundreds of firecrackers filled the air. The space station tilted to one side.

Harry's insides twisted. He had never

felt worse in his life. How would he tell Grace what happened?

The *Freedom* rose in the air just as there was a huge blast. The space station blew up behind them, in an explosion of fire and metal.

CHAPTER THIRTEEN

A. J. and Lev collapsed on the floor inside the shuttle *Independence*. They had made it in the nick of time.

The doors snapped shut behind them. The shuttle blasted away from the space station on full thruster power, just in time to escape the explosion.

The pilot got on the radio. "*Freedom*, the entire *Independence* crew is accounted for. We're even heavy one cosmonaut. How about you?"

Harry and the rest of the crew on the *Freedom* cheered. "We're all in one piece, *Independence*. Glad to hear you're still up and running," Watts radioed back.

The two shuttles rocketed on toward the

moon. Bear cranked up the music. Noonan tried to eat a floating tube of beef stew. Max hung upside down like a bat and slept. Harry, Chick, and Rockhound looked out the window at faraway planet Earth.

"Look at it," said Harry, "just floating there. All those people living on that ball. Right now all those lives are in our hands."

He got the chills and turned away. "If I keep thinking about it, I'll go crazy."

Through the windshield the men could see the moon getting larger. They could also see the asteroid, surrounded by rocks and ice, just beyond the moon.

Sharp got on the radio. "We have a visual of the target, Houston. Velocity thirty-three hundred miles per hour."

Back at Mission Control, Flight Director Clark sat at the console with two techs, Flip and Skip. Behind him, Dan Truman and General Kimsey were pacing back and forth.

The crews in the two shuttles could see

the surface of the moon rushing past. It looked close enough to touch.

"Closing on the dark side," Watts radioed Houston. "Sixty-four seconds on the mark."

"Eighteen seconds to radio interrupt," Skip radioed back. When the shuttles were on the other side of the moon, NASA would lose contact with them for several minutes.

Sharp and Watts prepared to slingshot around the moon and land on the asteroid.

"Rockets ready, on your mark," Watts spoke into the radio.

"See you on the other side," Truman said. Clark gave him a nod. "Radio contact terminated. We're out."

The *Freedom* and the *Independence* fired their boosters and shot forward. They whipped around the moon's dark side at a speed no human had ever known.

The crew got hit with their first G-forces. They were jammed back into their seats.

Harry felt like his arms weighed three hundred pounds and an elephant was sitting on his chest. Some of the guys passed out.

Watts could hardly speak. She read the speed off the gauge through clenched teeth.

"Fourteen thousand . . . sixteen thousand . . . twenty-two thousand miles per hour."

The G-forces got worse. They felt like their bodies were being turned inside out. Their cheeks and lips were flattened against their skulls, and they could barely breathe.

Suddenly, they saw the asteroid close up. Harry's heart lodged in his throat. The thing was gigantic. It was surrounded by ice chunks, pebbles, boulders, and icebergs as big as houses. They zoomed toward it.

"This is Houston. Come in *Freedom*. Come in *Independence*." It was Flight Director Clark's voice. They were in radio contact again.

Bang! Bang! Bang! Pebbles and ice chunks pelted the *Freedom*'s windshield.

Bang! Flying rocks took out the rear thruster of the *Independence*. Fuel spewed out in a blue flame. The shuttle spun out of control.

In the cockpit, Davis radioed Houston. "Mayday! Mayday! We're not going to make it. We're going down!"

The two shuttles nearly collided. Sharp pulled away just in time. Then the *Freedom* was hit by a huge ice boulder. Harry, Oscar, and Rockhound were thrown from side to side in the zero-gravity cabin.

A rock tore through the roof of the *Independence*. Ceiling panels filled with electrical wires broke free. In the cargo bay, mack trannies, pipes, and drill bits spun around.

Tucker was still on the radio. "Mayday, Houston. Mayday!"

Truman, Clark, and the others at

Mission Control could only listen. There was nothing they could do.

The *Independence* twirled down faster and faster, spewing smoke. Trannies, pipes, and metal splinters flew out of the hole in the roof and hit the *Freedom*'s nose.

The *Independence* slammed hard into the asteroid's surface. The ceiling split open like a can of tuna. The cabin filled with ice and rocks.

The wreck of the *Independence* skipped, bounced, and finally skidded to a stop. The radio crackled and was silent.

CHAPTER FOURTEEN

The *Freedom* swooped over a craggy slope on the asteroid's surface. Then it slammed down hard. Harry and his team were smashed around in their seats.

"Check the systems," Sharp told Watts. "Make sure we can still get off this rock."

Harry and his team tore off their harnesses. "Where's the other shuttle?" Rockhound asked nervously.

"*Independence* is off the grid," Sharp replied.

"Off the grid?" Rockhound echoed. "What's that mean?"

Gruber, the bomb specialist, spoke softly. "You saw it. She's gone."

The guys started freaking out. Harry

took charge. "Let's do what we gotta do and get outta here," he said.

While Sharp and Watts checked the equipment and tried to get the radio going, the guys suited up. Max got into the Armadillo.

Harry walked down the ramp first, onto the asteroid. The shuttle had landed in a small, dark valley, turned away from the earth and the sun. The moon was huge on the far horizon.

"Wow, Harry, we're in space," Rockhound said.

"We'll sightsee later," Harry told him. "Let's go."

The crew started drilling. Harry and Chick worked the drill arm and watched the depth and speed gauges.

The first ten feet went fine. They went to fifteen feet . . . then twenty.

Clank! Clank! Clank!

"What was that?" Harry asked.

Ksssssshhhhh-Booommm! The bit broke apart. The drill died.

Harry's heart thudded in his chest. "We've all seen bits get fried before," he said.

"Not after twenty feet," Chick shot back.

"Well, now we have!" Harry shouted. "Get that sorry look off your face! Let's re-bit this as fast as we can—move!"

In the cockpit, Watts got the radio to light up. "Houston, this is *Freedom*. Do you read?"

There were cheers and applause at Mission Control. "*Freedom*! Yes! God bless *Freedom*!" Truman radioed back.

Outside, Harry and his crew had started drilling again. They went to twenty-five feet, and then . . .

Clang-Clang-Boom! The bit was chewed again. They were all in shock.

"Get another bit on this thing," Harry barked. "Let's go!"

The crew got the third bit in place, and

drilling started up again. The drill spun faster and faster. Then suddenly it slowed down. *Boom*! The tranny blew. Metal scraps shot everywhere.

Harry checked his watch. "We're way behind," he muttered.

"Meet me in the shuttle," Harry said to Sharp.

Inside the shuttle, Harry explained the problems. He wanted Sharp to help replace the transmission.

"We're supposed to be at two hundred feet," said Sharp. "How deep are we?"

"Not as deep as we will be when you stop asking questions that waste my time," Harry replied.

"I need a depth to report," Sharp insisted.

"Fifty-seven feet!" Harry snapped. "We landed on a metal plate. Once we get through it, it'll go as fast as any other job."

Sharp was already on the cockpit radio,

talking to Mission Control, telling them that Harry and his crew couldn't stop the asteroid from hitting the earth. "Transmission change, twenty minutes, puts drilling final at ten hours. That's four hours past Zero Barrier!"

Harry ripped the radio out of his hands and started talking. "This is the way drilling goes sometimes. You can't panic."

He dropped the radio and turned to Sharp. "Now I need you back in the cargo bay to help drag that transmission out there."

Sharp didn't move. "You can't do it. I knew it was a mistake to bring you and your crew here."

Harry looked at the colonel with disgust. "You stay here. You supervise and report. I'll do the real work."

Harry pushed past Colonel Sharp and walked into the cargo bay. There he saw something that made his heart beat faster.

It was the clock on the bomb. The count-down had started. In four minutes, the thing would blow.

"Sharp! Get back here!" he yelled.

Sharp came running in. When he saw the clock counting down, he went wild. "Watts! Get the shuttle ready to e-vac in two minutes!" he screamed.

"I don't know if we can fire up in time!" the pilot yelled back.

Sharp grabbed the bomb. "They're detonating this thing from earth!" he told Harry. "We gotta drop it and go!"

"No!" said Harry. "Without putting this bomb down eight hundred feet, blowing it up is just a real expensive fireworks show. Houston might not think we can drill that hole, but *I* do."

From the cockpit, Watts shouted some bad news. "Central generator's not coming back on-line. Sharp, we are not going to make it!"

CHAPTER FIFTEEN

"This thing's gonna blow!" Sharp said. "We gotta get the bomb off this ship!"

Harry shook his head. "Stop the clock."

From the cockpit Watts shouted, "We have full power!"

Just then the bomb counter froze at 1:09. "It could start up again," Sharp said. "That might've been a warning."

Harry lunged at Sharp and grabbed him hard. "That's why you're gonna take apart that bomb right now. I don't want any more surprises."

"Forty-five seconds to engines!" Watts called.

Suddenly the bomb's countdown started again. 1:02 . . . 1:01 . . .

Sharp struggled to get away from Harry, but he couldn't. Harry looked him in the eye. "Right now you can follow an order or you can do the right thing," he said. "We can beat this thing! Please."

"Let me see it in your eyes," Sharp said. "Swear you can do it."

"I swear," Harry replied.

"All right," Sharp told him. "I'll disobey the order. I'll take the heat. I just hope I can shut it off."

Harry let go of him, and Sharp began working furiously to dismantle the bomb. He removed the outer panels, hit buttons, pulled wires. He didn't notice when a microchip from inside the bomb fell through the floor grating.

The clock kept counting down . . . 05 . . . 04 . . . 03 . . . Sharp kept working as fast as he could. Sweat beaded up on his forehead. Harry held his breath.

The timer shut off at two seconds.

Harry got on the radio. "Houston, you have a problem. You see, I promised my daughter I'm coming home! Now, I don't know what you are doing down there but we got a hole to dig up here."

With Gruber's help Harry and Sharp got the new transmission in place. They started the drill up again.

"You know the job," Harry said to his crew. "We got two hours to rip through this plate and chew seven hundred feet. Let's make this one work!"

The drill began grinding, digging into the metal plate. The ground trembled.

Sharp figured a quake was coming. "These tremblers are getting worse," he said.

Max was sweating buckets. The engine was roaring.

"Harry!" Chick called. "I think we broke through the plate!"

Harry's heart leaped. "Hang in there,

Max!" He shouted. "We're at one hundred fifty feet. Keep it up, my man!"

The drilling started going faster. Stacks of pipe and rock started piling up around the hole. The guys didn't stop for a second.

Suddenly, the ground began to split open right under their feet. Harry saw the drill arm kick, then kick again, harder.

"Max, pull the drill! Clear the hole now!" He screamed.

A huge trembler rocked the valley. Chick pulled Harry away from the drilling hole just as *Ka-blam*! There was a huge explosion. Pipe flew everywhere. The whole Armadillo blew skyward.

Then suddenly the quake was over. The crew stood there in silence.

Watts headed into the shuttle and radioed Mission Control. "Houston . . . this is *Freedom*. We've lost the Armadillo. Drilling terminated. Unsuccessful."

CHAPTER SIXTEEN

The sun was creeping over the asteroid's far horizon as A. J. rumbled over a little hill in his Armadillo. He and Lev had managed to pull it out of the twisted wreck of the *Independence*. They'd managed to pull Bear out, too. His foot had been badly hurt in the crash. The three of them were the only ones left of the *Independence* crew.

While A. J. drove, Lev and Bear bounced along in the back. Bear gritted his teeth in pain.

A. J. checked the locator beacon on the control panel. He turned toward the signal. He hoped it would lead them to Harry and the crew of the *Freedom*. If they didn't find the other shuttle, they'd never get off the asteroid.

"I never thought I'd be in a place as bad as Outer Mongolia," A. J. said. "That was where I did my second job with Harry."

"You think Outer Mongolia is bad?" Lev asked. "You should try Siberia. It's so cold there it hurts."

Suddenly A. J. slammed on the brakes. They were at the edge of a ridge. Beyond was a fifty-foot drop. There was no way around it.

Lev got out and climbed on top of the Armadillo. A. J. walked out front, looking for a way down. He didn't see one.

"This is the worst situation ever," Lev said. "I'm telling you, you took the wrong road."

"*Road?* What *road?*" A. J. sputtered. "Is there some *map* you're not showing me?" He picked up a rock and threw it in disgust. The rock never landed, it just floated away.

A. J. got an idea. If they couldn't go around the gully, they'd have to go over it.

"Ever hear of Evil Knievel?" he asked Lev.

The cosmonaut stared at him blankly. The two of them got back in the Armadillo.

A. J. jammed the Armadillo in reverse. The tires skidded. A. J. took a deep breath, then looked at Lev.

Lev repeated the plan. "Thrusters off when we make jump. Thrusters on for to come down."

"This is going to work. Say it," A. J. ordered.

"I am not so sure. But if we make this . . . you will be hero like me."

"That's fair," A. J. said. Then he zoomed right for the edge of the gully as he turned off the pro-gravity thrusters.

The Armadillo shot over the gully, clearing it with plenty to spare. Lev pushed the thruster fire switch. Nothing happened.

Lev looked down. They were going higher and higher. "Jets not firing!" he gasped. "We are floating to space!" He pulled himself out of his seat and rushed to the air lock.

A. J.'s heart pounded. "You're climbing outside!"

"I am saving your American life!" Lev told him. He scrambled out onto the roof and crawled to the thruster port. It was caked with ice. Lev aimed a torch at it and pressed the button.

"Please work, please," he begged.

The valve sputtered. Lev mumbled something in Russian.

"Lev, incoming!" A. J. called, just as floating rocks peppered the roof of the Armadillo. Lev rolled, dodging the hits, barely hanging on.

A side-mounted fuel canister exploded, sending Lev grabbing for the tow winch cable. The whole vehicle was spinning end over end with Lev hanging on underneath. The ground was whizzing by, a hundred feet below.

A. J. pushed the fire button and the thrusters engaged. Lev hung on for his life as the wheels of the Armadillo slammed into the surface of the asteroid. They did it!

A. J. popped his head out of the Armadillo and looked at Lev, sprawled fifty feet behind him. The cosmonaut was covered with dirt and grime. A grin spread over his face. It was the first time A. J. had seen him smile.

CHAPTER SEVENTEEN

A light washed across Harry's space suit. He turned and looked into the blazing headlights of the second Armadillo. Inside the shuttle, Watts got on the radio again.

"Houston, you're not gonna believe this! The Armadillo! The other Armadillo! It's here!"

Harry couldn't believe his eyes as A. J. popped out of the roof hatch. "There's a great little Italian place like three miles that way," he joked.

Harry couldn't help smiling. "Ya feel like helping us drill a hole?"

The grin faded from A. J.'s face. "I've only got Bear and the cosmonaut with me. The others didn't make it."

"We'll take whoever we can get," Harry said.

"Then let's get dirty."

Watts radioed the good news to Mission Control. "Houston, drilling has recommenced."

Wind pounded the guys as they worked. Suddenly, the ground began to tremble again. Harry saw the drill arm jump.

"Slow it down!" he called to A. J.

A. J. kept going. "Harry, if you're ever gonna trust me, do it now! We can't pull back. The bit'll get stuck and the whole thing will blow!"

"I don't think the arm can take the pressure," Harry said.

"If the bit gets chewed we'll replace it! If the tranny blows we'll throw on another one!"

"I got some news for ya!" Harry said. "We're all out of bits and trannies!"

"What?!" A. J. gasped. His mind reeled. "Oh, no!"

The Armadillo was bucking. Sharp, Bear, and Gruber all stared at Harry, waiting to see what he would do. He was in charge.

"A. J.! All right, I'm trusting you on this," Harry said after a moment.

A. J. panicked. What if he was wrong? "Now wait a second!" he said hurriedly.

Harry stood behind his decision. "Kid, this is on your shoulders," he said. "Do it! Punch it!"

A. J. gritted his teeth. He drove the bit hard and fast. The drill roared. The pressure gauge kept jumping, but the drill arm held. They were racing against time.

Harry held his breath as he kept his eyes glued to the depth gauge. Finally the needle hit 804 feet.

"A. J.! You did it!" Harry whooped. "Let's start pulling pipe!"

Watts radioed the news. "Houston, we're at eight hundred feet."

Cheers erupted at Mission Control.

CHAPTER EIGHTEEN

Sharp and Gruber finished putting the bomb back together. "We're almost ready to drop this thing in," Sharp said.

Harry, Bear, and A. J. were running the drill full speed in reverse. They were trying to pull it out of the ground as fast as they could.

Suddenly, a wrench fell out of Bear's hand. It dropped into the turbine engine. The drill made a horrible grinding noise. Then it jammed back down into the hole, buckling and twisting.

Harry walked to the edge of the hole. Fifty feet down there was a mess of twisted metal and mangled pipe. They had to clear the hole to put the bomb down deep enough.

"Run me out some cable," Harry told A. J.

"You're not going down there," A. J. said.

"Says who?" Harry started running the cable out himself.

"I'm a better climber than you and I don't know how many decades younger," A. J. said.

Harry glared at him. Then he handed him the cable. "You better start climbing."

A. J. went into the hole with a handheld cutter and a length of rope. Pipes were mashed and bent, stabbed into the walls.

The ground rumbled. A. J. was rattled around as he tied the rope to the pipes.

The tremor was building. Then the earthquake hit full force. It was the biggest one yet.

A. J. was trying to climb out of the hole. A windstorm of pebbles smashed into his face shield.

Whooossshh! The noise grew louder and louder. Harry looked across the valley floor and saw a hundred-foot methane geyser erupt. Plumes of green gas rocketed into space. Another geyser erupted, then another and another.

Harry turned and saw A. J. shoot out of the hole. His safety line stretched tight, then broke. A. J. flew seventy feet off the ground.Harry grabbed the end of the cable just in time to save A. J. from drifting into space.

Chunks of the asteroid broke free and started rolling faster and faster. A huge ice boulder rolled over A. J.'s safety line and yanked him toward the ground.

Sharp saw it happen. He jumped into the Armadillo and roared toward the ice boulder. The Armadillo rammed it just before it hit A. J.

A. J. was safe, but only for a moment. The grappling hook at the end of the safety line was stuck in the rolling boulder. The slack in the line ran out quickly.

Whomp! A. J. was slammed into a rock. All the wind was knocked out of him. He managed to release his harness. The rock rolled away as A. J. watched with relief. He could have been crushed.

Meanwhile, the biggest piece of jagged rock was rolling toward Harry and Chick, getting closer and closer. The two of them looked around wildly. There was nowhere to turn.

Just in time, Harry pulled Chick into a tiny hole. The rock rolled right over the two of them, nearly skimming their face shields. They could hardly believe they had escaped being hit.

Finally, the quake stopped. Harry and Chick stood up. Harry stumbled toward the hole and looked inside. The metal and pipe had been blown out. It was clear.

He walked over to Sharp, who was holding the bomb. A. J. was standing beside him. Sharp looked horrified. "What's wrong now?" Harry asked.

"The timer, the remote, the whole thing's dead. Something must've gotten fried when we took it apart," Sharp replied.

"Sharp, how do we detonate this thing?" Harry asked.

Sharp hesitated. "Now . . . the only way is . . . manually."

A. J. went pale. "You mean . . . by hand?"

Harry felt a chill race up his spine. "He means one of us has to stay."

CHAPTER NINETEEN

"It's settled. I'm the guy who gets to save the earth," A. J. said calmly. The crew was gathered in the cabin of the *Freedom*. They had just drawn straws to decide who would stay on the asteroid and set off the bomb. A. J. had drawn the shortest straw.

Sharp showed A. J. how to detonate the bomb. Harry watched. His stomach was tied in knots. He knew Grace loved A. J., and he had promised to get him back to her.

A. J. turned to Harry. "Do me a favor," he said in a choked voice. "Tell Grace I miss her. Would you do that?"

"No," Harry said. He snatched his own mission patch from his space suit and shoved it into one of A. J.'s pockets. "Give that to Truman," he said. Then he ripped A. J.'s air tubes apart. Now A. J. couldn't breathe outside the shuttle. He started to gasp.

Harry grabbed the detonator from A. J.'s hands. "This time it's my turn," he said. He shoved A. J. into the shuttle's elevator.

A. J. looked through the window. "This is my job! I'm gonna get another suit!"

Their eyes locked. "Go take care of Grace," Harry said. "Go be the husband she deserves." Then he hit a button and the elevator sucked A. J. into the shuttle.

A moment later the elevator doors opened in the airlock. A. J. fell out at Chick's feet.

Outside, Harry walked to the Armadillo and climbed in. He called Grace back at Mission Control. He stared into the camera.

"I know I promised I was coming home . . . but . . . Grace, I gotta break that promise."

Tears welled up in Grace's eyes. "Why?"

Harry was fighting back his own tears. "Honey, stop. Listen to me, there isn't much time. I just want to tell you that I'm here because I love you."

"We're two peas in a pod," said Grace. "Everything good I got from you and I need you to know that, 'cause right now I'm scared."

Harry looked down at the earth. "There won't be anything to be scared of soon, and don't be scared for me. I'll be just fine. It's so beautiful up here."

Tears were rolling down Grace's cheeks. She knew she would never see her father on earth again.

"I wish I could walk you down the aisle," Harry said. "I'll look in on you from time to time. I love you, Gracie."

Harry disconnected the video link. Grace watched Harry's face fade from the screen.

CHAPTER TWENTY

At Mission Control the clock was counting down the minutes to Zero Barrier. 1:34 . . . 1:32 . . . 1:31.

Sharp and Watts were in the cockpit of the shuttle *Freedom*, preparing for takeoff. A. J., Rockhound, Chick, and Lev were in the cabin, strapped into their seats.

"Initiate thrusters," Sharp ordered.

Watts hit the thruster button. Nothing happened. She hit it again. Then again.

"I just had it running!" she said through clenched teeth. The booster rockets sputtered and died.

Watts unbuckled and ran back toward the cargo bay. Lev unstrapped himself and went after her.

He caught up with Watts in the engine service hatch. She was trying to get the fuel valve open.

Lev crowded behind her. "Is stuck, yes?"

"Back off!" Watts ordered. "You don't know what you're doing."

Lev pulled her out of the way. "I spend year and a half on Russian space station. This is how I fix everything." He began hitting the valve with his wrench.

Suddenly, *Vroooommm!* The valve opened and the engine fired. Lev fell back into Watts' arms as the *Freedom* lurched.

On the asteroid's surface, Harry watched the *Freedom* lift off. It rose toward the moon.

Harry took a few deep breaths. Tears welled in his eyes. He watched the *Freedom* get smaller and smaller.

At Mission Control Dan Truman watched the time count down to Zero Barrier. There were only seconds left.

"Press the button, Stamper!" he prayed.

Up on the asteroid the winds were gusting badly. Harry raised the detonator to press the button.

Wham! Just below him three geysers of gas blew out of the ground. The detonator flew from Harry's hand as he was knocked backward into the drilling hole.

Harry's fingers gouged into the walls and his boots scrambled against the sides of the hole as he tried to stop falling. He gasped as a jagged edge of rock punctured his air supply hose.

In the *Freedom*'s cockpit, the voice of Flight Director Clark came over the radio. "*Freedom,* we're thirty seconds to Zero Barrier. Where's the detonation?"

"Something's wrong," Sharp muttered. "We gotta go back."

"There's no going back!" said Watts. "We won't have enough fuel to make it home."

They all knew that if the bomb didn't go off, they wouldn't have a home to go to. "Even if something's wrong, Harry won't quit," said A. J. "He doesn't know how."

A. J. was right. Harry managed to pull himself out of the hole. With geysers exploding all around him and the wind and dust flying, he managed to find the detonator.

Harry was gasping for air, and he was in a lot of pain. Tears welled up in his eyes as he took one last look at the beautiful earth. Home.

Time to Zero Barrier . . . 05 . . . 04 . . . 03 . . .

"I win," said Harry. He pressed the button.

The explosion split the asteroid in half. The two pieces flew apart. The shuttle was rocked by the blast.

"Harry Stamper, I love you, man," Bear whispered.

Chick looked down at the earth. "Look at her. She's safe now, but she also got a bit more lonely."

A. J. nodded with tears in his eyes.

On earth, farmers in a midwestern cornfield knew they were safe when they saw the brilliant flash in the sky. The explosion lit up the pyramids. Little children in India ran through the streets as it blazed overhead.

In Harry's house in Texas, Harry's father was spooning real pudding into his mouth when the bright flare filled the room. "That's my boy," he said.

CHAPTER TWENTY-ONE

The landing strip was crowded with ambulances, firetrucks, and vans from television stations. Reporters were swarming all over the place.

All eyes were turned skyward. Then the shuttle came into view, just a speck in the sky at first. The speck grew larger as the *Freedom* streaked toward the earth.

The shuttle was coming in for the landing too quickly. The guys were getting bounced around a lot. Things were shaking, rattling, and dropping all over the cabin. The crew didn't know if they would land in one piece.

Bang! The tires crashed down on the concrete. The shuttle skittered along, tilting and wobbling. The wheels screamed as the

Freedom sped down the runway.

Everyone in the crowd held their breath. Finally, the shuttle skidded to a stop.

Chick nearly jumped from his seat. "Get me outta this thing right now," he said.

"Guys, stay in your seats until they tell us what to do," Sharp told them. "There are a lot of people out there. It's gonna be a madhouse, so just sit tight, okay?"

Yeah, right, thought A. J. There's no way I'll just sit here. He turned to the others. "It's times like this you gotta ask yourself what Harry Stamper would do." He started unstrapping himself.

A moment later the emergency hatch doors exploded from their hinges and crashed onto the runway. Everyone stared in shock as A. J. and the rest of the crew started climbing out.

The men smiled and waved. The crowd clapped and cheered. The noise got louder and louder.

Lev leaned toward Rockhound. "I wonder if my family could get citizenship here?" he asked.

"Buddy, at this point your family could have their own talk show," Rockhound answered.

Everyone went nuts as the heroes came down the runway pumping their fists in the air. Security police had a hard job holding back the throngs of people. American flags were flying all around.

Grace saw A. J. at the same instant he saw her. They ran toward each other. Then they fell into each other's arms.

"He was a good man, Grace," A. J. said.

"I know," Grace answered.

Chick's son was in the crowd with his mother. He was cheering like mad. Finally, he couldn't wait any longer to welcome his dad home. He broke through the crowd and ran onto the landing strip. Security police chased after him.

Chick saw his son. "Leave him alone!" he told the police. Then he lifted his son high into the air as the crowd roared.

Colonel Sharp marched up to Grace and A. J. "Ms. Stamper, Colonel Roger Sharp, United States Air Force. Requesting permission to shake the hand of the daughter of the bravest man I've ever met."

Grace smiled and straightened up. The two shook hands.

A. J. noticed Dan Truman standing nearby. He handed him Harry's mission patch. "Harry wanted you to have this."

Truman's eyes teared up. He smiled at A. J. as he took the patch. "Thank you."

Arm in arm, Grace and A. J.stared up into the sky along with Colonel Sharp, Dan Truman, and the rest of the crowd. They all knew Harry Stamper was up there somewhere.

gear up for ARMAGEDDON

RECEIPT =

Special Offer

FREE GIFT

ARMAGEDDON movie heroes wear
SWISS ARMY SUNGLASSES
on their mission to save the world.

When you buy a pair of Swiss Army® Sunglasses
at any U.S. retail outlet and mail in the original
cash register receipt plus UPC label, we'll send you
a limited edition Victorinox® Original Swiss Army™ Knife
the Bladeless! **FREE!** It has five cool gadgets:
scissors, ball point pen, caplifter, screwdriver, key ring
with ARMAGEDDON printed on
the handle.

SHIELD YOUR EYES.
YOU'RE GONNA NEED THEM.